WITHDRAWN

To Mark, James, Joseph and Jessica
~ J H

LITTLE TIGER PRESS
An imprint of Magi Publications
1 The Coda Centre, 189 Munster Road, London SW6 6AW
www.littletigerpress.com

First published in Great Britain 2007

Text copyright © Julia Hubery 2007
Illustrations copyright © Sophy Williams 2007
Julia Hubery and Sophy Williams have asserted their rights to be identified
as the author and illustrator of this work under the Copyright, Designs and Patents Act, 1988

A CIP catalogue record for this book is available from the British Library

Printed in China

2 4 6 8 10 9 7 5 3 1

A Christmas Wish

JULIA HUBERY   SOPHY WILLIAMS

LITTLE TIGER PRESS
London

Gemma gazed up at the Christmas
tree. She'd watched excitedly as
Mum and Dad stood it up. She'd
cut the net, freed the branches . . .
and breathed in the magical
smell of Christmas.

At last it was time to unpack the
decorations. Gemma's brother Ty
danced round her knees impatiently.
"Ty, calm down or you'll POP!"
she laughed.

Gemma had told him all about the
shiny baubles, the glittering tinsel . . .
and her favourite, the leaping snow
deer, who sparkled like ice and sugar.

One by one – oh so carefully –
Gemma unwrapped the decorations.

At last she found the dusty box where
the snow deer slept. Ty spotted something
sparkly in the box, and reached out for it.
"Careful, Ty! Don't touch!" cried Gemma,
yanking the box away quickly – too quickly.
The snow deer fell from his hands . . .

There was the tiniest snap as
it hit the floor, and lay broken.
Now Gemma had no heart for
decorating the tree. Suddenly,
she hated Ty.

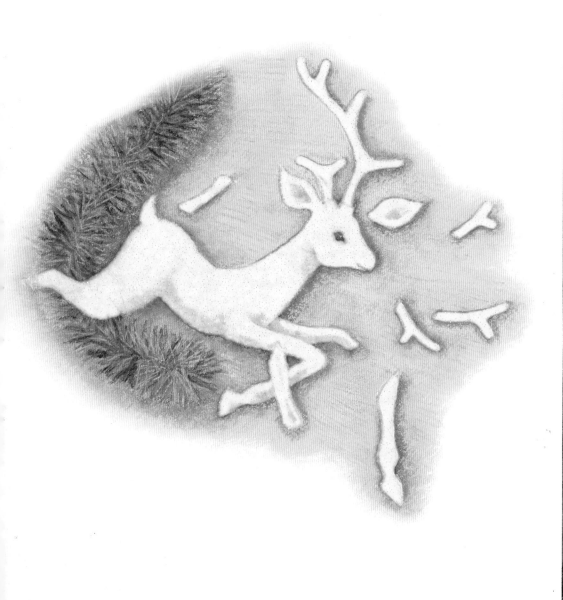

"Is something broken?" asked Mum.
"It's the snow deer, the one I really love,
my snow deer. Stupid Ty broke him to bits."
"It was an accident, Gem. You know how
excited he is."

Ty tried to say sorry. He brought his favourite teddy to Gemma. "Your teddy, Gemmie," he said. Gemma wouldn't look at Ty. She threw his teddy to the floor and stomped out of the room.

Gemma laid the snow deer on her pillow.
She remembered last Christmas: dark evenings,
sitting by the tree, dreaming with the snow deer . . .

. . . dreams where he carried her
through sparkling skies, high above
sleepy toy-town cities and patchwork
fields . . .

. . . then higher still, riding a wild snowstorm
   to the ice palaces of the North Pole. In crystal
   halls shimmering with the light of a thousand
   fairies they danced to a blaze of star-music,
   spinning and whirling till the stars fell asleep,
   one by one.

"Ty would have loved flying with the snow deer," thought Gemma. She remembered last Christmas Eve. Ty had bounced into her room in the middle of the night, because he wanted to see Santa's reindeer.

Then he had snuggled up with Gemma
like a big teddy bear.

"But he's better than a teddy – he hugs you
back!" thought Gemma. She began to feel
she'd been mean to Ty.

Gemma wondered how late
it was. It was very quiet. She
opened the door, and nearly
fell over something. On the
floor was a badly-wrapped
parcel, and a little card with
a big wobbly "sorry".

It was a pot of glue.
"To mend the snow deer!"
Gemma laughed.

Gemma crept downstairs.
"Look what Ty gave me," she whispered.
Working patiently, Mum and Gemma
stuck the snow deer back together.

"Now, it really is bedtime," said Mum.
But Gemma had one more thing to do.
She took the snow deer into Ty's room . . .

"Ty," she whispered, and the snow deer
flew down to brush his cheek with a kiss.
"He's better now," said Gemma. "Let's make a
Christmas wish. Maybe, just maybe, he'll fly
us to the stars."

Moonbeams kissed their sleepy heads as they
closed their eyes tight and wished . . .

. . . and together they flew high
above the sleepy towns into
the magical, velvet night.